Mercy Watson Fights Crime

Kate DiCamillo

Mercy Watson Fights Crime

illustrated by Chris Van Dusen

CANDLEWICK PRESS
CAMBRIDGE, MASSACHUSETTS

First edition 2006

Library of Congress Cataloging-in-Publication Data
DiCamillo, Kate.
Mercy Watson fights crime / Kate DiCamillo ; illustrated by Chris Van Dusen.
—1st ed.
p. cm.
Summary: Mercy the pig's love of buttered toast leads to the capture of a small thief who would rather be a cowboy.
ISBN-13: 978-0-7636-2590-0
ISBN-10: 0-7636-2590-6
[1. Pigs—Fiction. 2. Burglary—Fiction. 3. Humorous stories.]
I. Van Dusen, Chris, ill. II. Title
PZ7.D5455Mdf2006
[Fic]—dc22 2005053639

6 8 10 9 7

Printed in China

This book was typeset in Mrs. Eaves.
The illustrations were done in gouache.

Candlewick Press
2067 Massachusetts Avenue
Cambridge, Massachusetts 02140

visit us at www.candlewick.com

For Tracey Priebe Bailey,
who continues to laugh
K. D.

For Lauren and Sarah,
two sweet, little, silly girls
C. V.

Chapter 1

Mr. Watson and Mrs. Watson have a pig named Mercy.

Each night, they sing the pig to sleep.

Then they go to bed.

"Good night, my dear," says Mr. Watson.

"Good night, my darling," says Mrs. Watson.

"Oink," says Mercy.

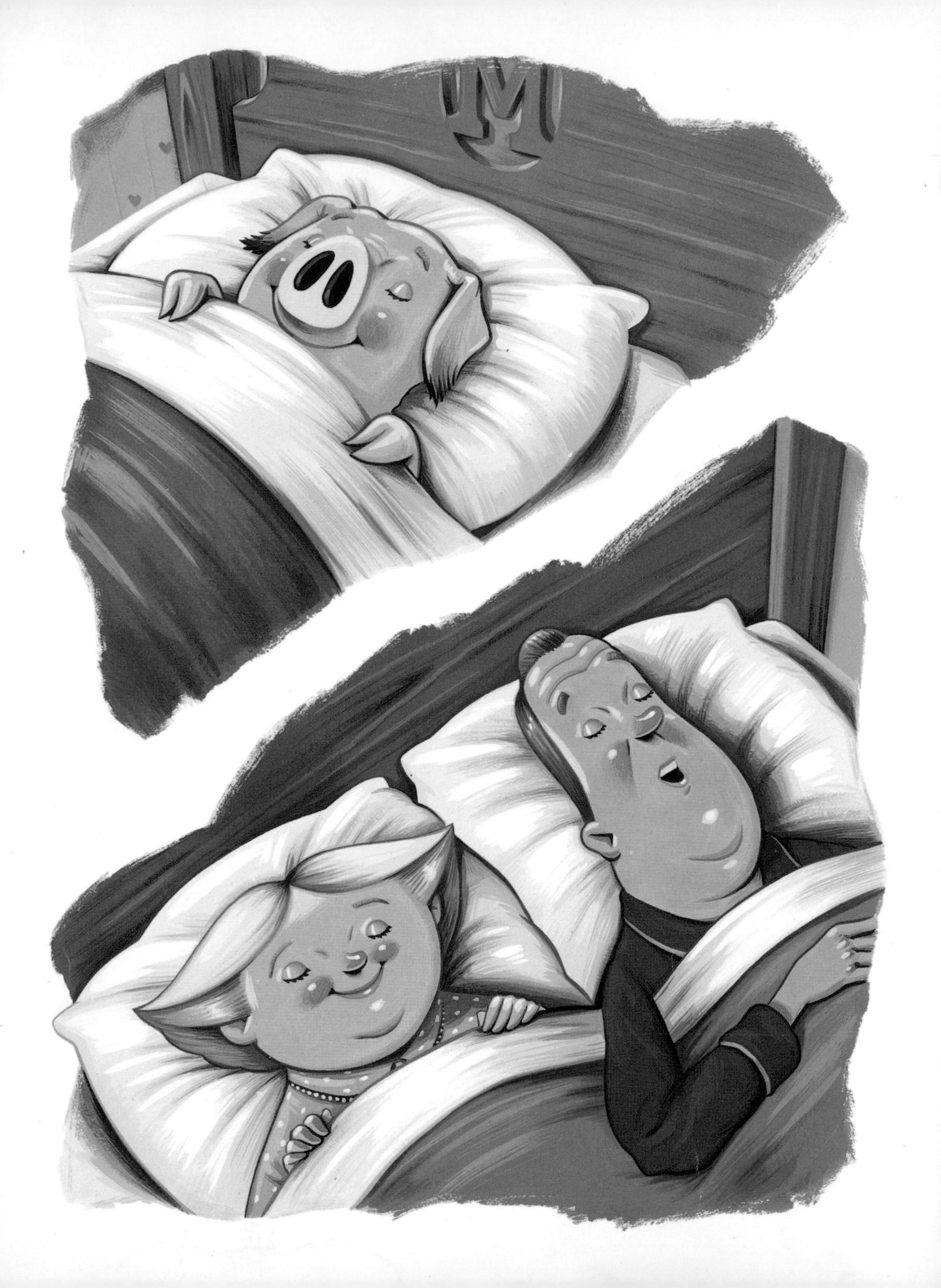

Most nights, Mr. Watson and Mrs. Watson and Mercy all sleep soundly in their beds.

But there was one night when they did not.

Chapter 2

Leroy Ninker was a small man.

He was a small man with a big dream.

Leroy Ninker wanted to be a cowboy.

But in the meantime, he was a thief.

He was a thief in the kitchen at 54 Deckawoo Drive.

Leroy Ninker was robbing the Watsons.

"Yippie-i-oh," sang Leroy, "everything must go!"

He grabbed hold of the toaster.

He pulled it across the counter toward him.

Screeeeeech, went the toaster.

"Shhhh," said Leroy.

He tossed the toaster into his bag.

Clannngggg, went the toaster.

"Shhhh," said Leroy again.

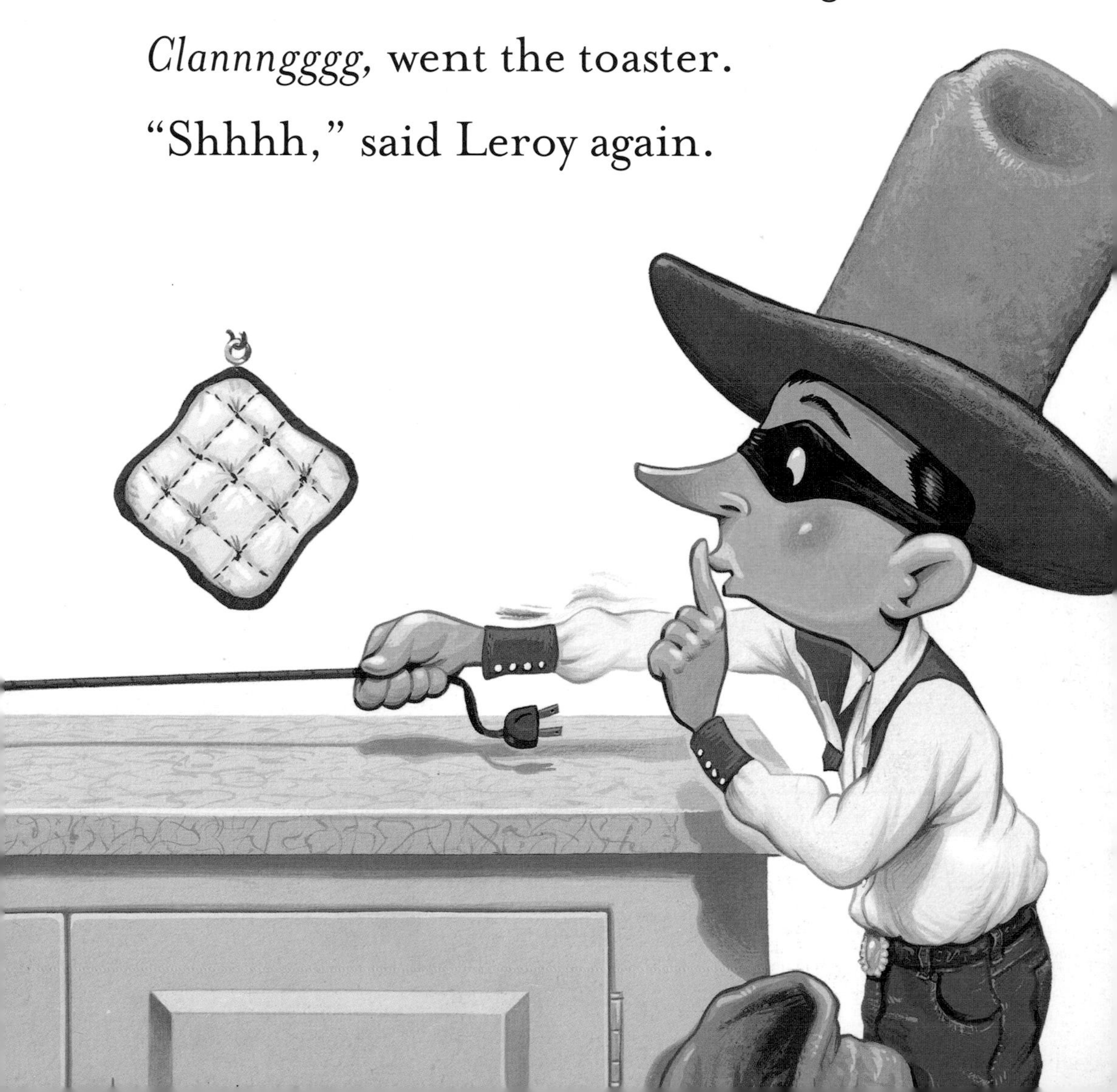

Chapter 3

Screeeeeechh

Mercy woke up.

Screeeeeech was the sound the toaster made when it was being pulled across the kitchen counter!

Mercy Watson loved toast.

She particularly loved toast with a great deal of butter on it.

Mercy got out of bed.

She pricked up her ears.

She listened.

Mercy heard Mr. Watson snoring. She heard Mrs. Watson snoring. Who was downstairs making toast? Mercy went to the top of the stairs. She looked down into the darkness. *Clannngggg,* went the toaster. *Clannngggg* was the sound the toaster made when Mrs. Watson turned it upside down to clean out all the crumbs!

Somebody was making toast.

Mercy went down the dark, dark stairs.

She headed for the kitchen.

Chapter 4

Leroy Ninker grabbed the blender.

He grabbed the clock.

He grabbed the cookie jar.

"Yippie-i-oh," he sang as he worked, "in you go!"

He grabbed the juicer.

He grabbed the teapot.

He grabbed the waffle iron.

And then Leroy Ninker heard a noise.

He turned around.

"Yippie-i—" sang Leroy, "uh-oh."

Chapter 5

Mercy looked around.

She did not see the toaster.

She did not see the bread.

She did not see the butter.

Instead, Mercy saw a little man wearing a big hat.

He was not making toast.

Mercy was very disappointed.

She was also very tired.

She yawned.

"Good pig," said the man.

He nodded.

Mercy lay down.

She yawned again.

"Nice pig," said the little man.

Mercy closed her eyes.

"Yippie-i-oh," the man sang softly, "off to sleep you go."

Z
Z
Z

Chapter 6

That there," whispered Leroy, "is a big pig."

He reached into his shirt pocket.

He pulled out a Butter Barrel candy.

He unwrapped the candy and put it in his mouth.

Hmm, Leroy thought. *It might be a good idea for this cowboy to hit the trail.*

He picked up his bag.

He stopped.

"Aw, shucks," said Leroy.

The pig was blocking his way.

"There's no room to go around the pig," said Leroy. "There's no room to go under the pig. Guess I got to go over the pig."

Leroy stepped forward.

He flung one leg over the sleeping pig.

The pig moved.

Leroy Ninker froze.

Chapter 7

Mercy woke up.

"Oink?" she said.

"Easy now," said a voice.

Mercy looked out of the corner of her eye.

The little man was on her back!

Mercy stood up.

"Steady, girl," said the little man.

Mercy shook herself.

The little man slid forward.

"Whoa there," he said.

Mercy smelled something.

What was it?

Butter!

Mercy looked around the kitchen.

No bread.

No toaster.

But she definitely smelled butter.

Maybe someone next door was making sugar cookies!

"Oink!" said Mercy.

She galloped out the open door.

She galloped toward the Lincoln Sisters' house.

"Yippie-i-oh!" shouted Leroy Ninker. "Away we go!"

Chapter 8

Upstairs at 54 Deckawoo Drive, Mrs. Watson woke up.

"Mr. Watson?" she said.

"Mmmphh," said Mr. Watson.

"Did you hear a noise?" said Mrs. Watson.

"What sort of a noise, dear?"

"A 'yippie-i-oh' sort of noise," said Mrs. Watson.

"No, I did not hear a 'yippie-i-oh' sort of noise," said Mr. Watson. "You were dreaming, my dear."

"I was?" said Mrs. Watson.

"You were," said Mr. Watson. "Go back to sleep."

Mrs. Watson got out of bed.

"I think that I will go and check on Mercy," she said. "And then I will go back to sleep."

"Excellent," mumbled Mr. Watson. "A top-notch plan, my dear."

Mr. Watson started to snore.

Chapter 9

Inside the Lincoln Sisters' house, Baby Lincoln woke up.

She went into her sister Eugenia's room.

"Sister, wake up," Baby said. "There is somebody outside shouting 'Yippie-i-oh.'"

"Did you have pie before bed again?" asked Eugenia.

"I did not," said Baby.

"I think you did," said Eugenia.

"I did not," said Baby.

"Go back to your room immediately," said Eugenia.

"Yes, Sister," said Baby.

Baby went back to her room.

She got into her bed.

She heard another "yippie-i-oh."

"Oh, dear," said Baby. "I wish I had not eaten that pie."

Chapter 10

"Baby!" shouted Eugenia. "Come back here immediately."

Baby got out of bed.

She went into Eugenia's room.

"Yes, Sister?" said Baby.

"Did you hear that noise?" said Eugenia.

"Was it a 'yippie-i-oh,' Sister?"

"It was," said Eugenia.

"You are dreaming," said Baby.

"Nonsense," said Eugenia. "Open the curtain."

Baby opened the curtain.

Together, the Lincoln Sisters watched Mercy gallop across the lawn.

They watched the little man on her back take his cowboy hat off and wave it over his head.

"Yippie-i-oh!" the little man shouted.

"That pig is disturbing the peace," said Eugenia. "And so is the cowboy riding her. I am calling the police."

"Oh, Sister," said Baby, "are you sure it's not a dream?"

"It's a nightmare," said Eugenia. "That is what it is."

Chapter 11

Next door, Mrs. Watson discovered that Mercy was not in her bed.

"Mr. Watson," she shouted, "come at once!"

Mr. Watson came at once.

"Mercy is not here," said Mrs. Watson.

"Are you certain?" asked Mr. Watson. "Have you looked under the bed?"

Mrs. Watson bent over.

She looked under the bed.

"She is not there," said Mrs. Watson.

Mr. and Mrs. Watson stood together in Mercy's room.

"What should we do?" asked Mrs. Watson.

"Yippie-i-oh!"

"It's that noise again," said Mrs. Watson.

Mr. Watson went to the window.

He opened the curtain.

He looked outside.

"Mrs. Watson," said Mr. Watson, "we must call the fire department immediately. It's an emergency!"

Chapter 12

In reality, Leroy Ninker was a small thief on the back of a big pig.

But in Leroy's mind, he was a cowboy riding a bucking bronco in the Wild West.

"Being a cowboy is hard work," said Leroy Ninker. "I need some refreshment."

Leroy reached into his shirt pocket.

He grabbed hold of a Butter Barrel candy.

He unwrapped it with one hand.

He put it in his mouth.

"Ah," said Leroy Ninker, "this is the life."

But just then, the pig kicked up her heels.

The pig bucked.

The pig reared.

Leroy Ninker lost his grip.

"Yippie—" said Leroy.

He flew through the air.

"I—" said Leroy.

He landed on his back.

"Oh!" said Leroy Ninker.

Chapter 13

Mercy sniffed.

There was that delightful smell again!

Butter!

Where was it coming from?

She looked around.

She saw the little man lying on the ground.

She sniffed his face.

"Hee-hee," the little man said. "That tickles."

Mercy snuffled the man's shirt.

"Hee-hee," he said again.

In order to snuffle the man better, Mercy sat on top of him.

"Hee-hee. Get off me," said the man.

Mercy put her snout in the man's shirt pocket.

She snuffled some more.

"Oh, hee-hee," said the little man. "Help."

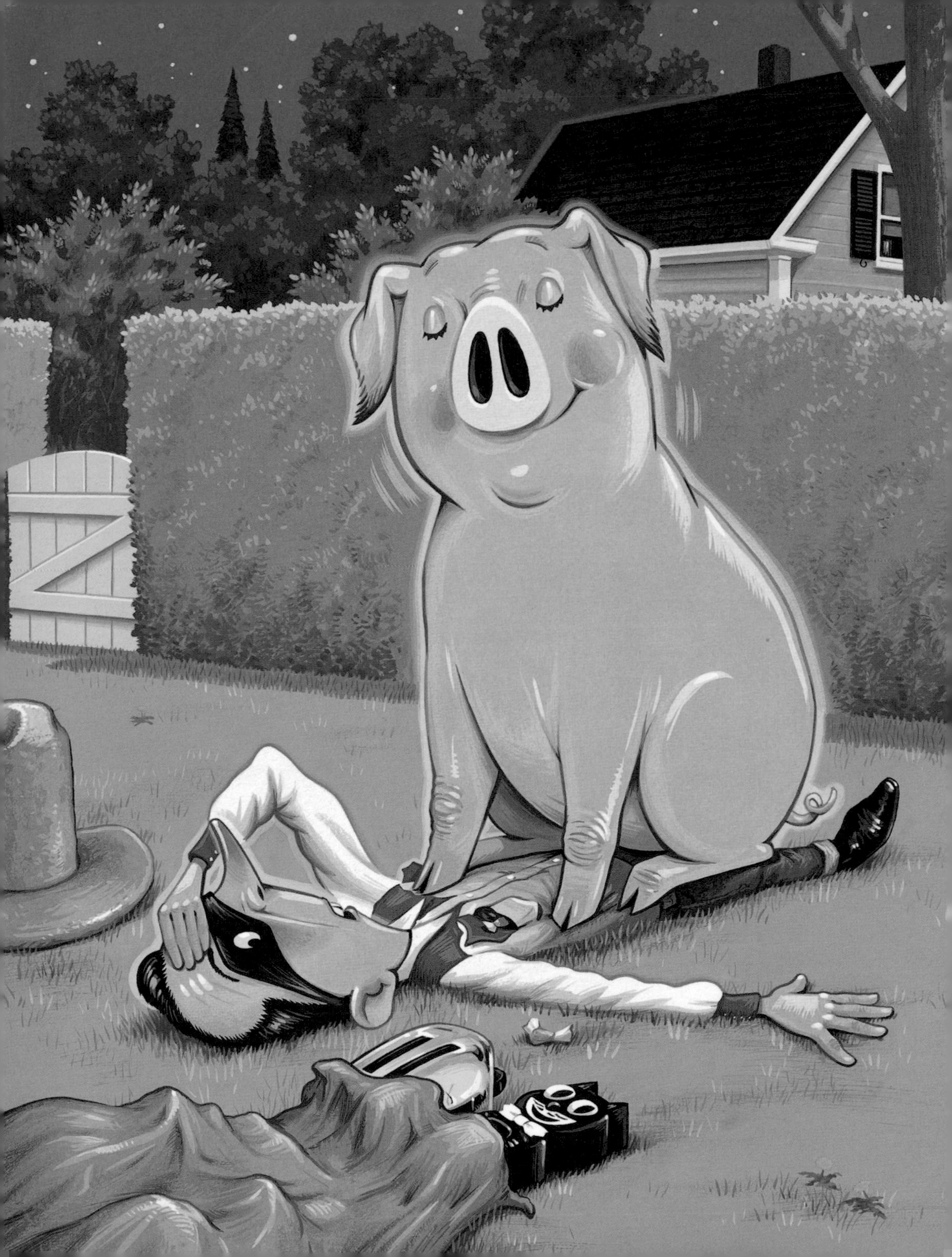

Mercy found a piece of candy.

She bit into it.

It was sweet.

It was lovely.

It was very, very buttery.

Mercy sat on top of the little man and chewed.

A siren wailed.

"Aw, shucks," said the man.

Chapter 14

The fire department arrived first.

"We have been to this house before," said the fireman named Ned.

"You are right," said the fireman named Lorenzo. "This is the house with the pig."

"And the toast," said Ned. "We ate toast at this house."

"I see the pig," said Lorenzo.

He pointed at Mercy.

"The pig is sitting on somebody."

"Good grief," said Ned.

Ned and Lorenzo got out of the fire truck.

They saw Mr. and Mrs. Watson running out the front door of their house.

They saw Eugenia Lincoln and Baby Lincoln running out the front door of their house.

"This is an interesting job, isn't it?" said Ned.

"Very interesting," said Lorenzo.

Chapter 15

Officer Tomilello pulled into the driveway of 54 Deckawoo Drive.

In the yard, he saw two firemen, three women in nightgowns, and one man in pajamas.

They were all gathered around a pig.

"Is that the same pig I caught driving a convertible?" he asked himself.

POLICE

"It is," he answered himself. "It is exactly the same pig."

Officer Tomilello squinted.

"Is that pig sitting on top of somebody?" Officer Tomilello asked himself.

"That certainly looks to be the case," he answered himself.

"Officer, Officer!" shouted Baby. "Come quickly. Mercy has caught a thief!"

Mr. Watson and Mrs. Watson and Eugenia Lincoln and Baby Lincoln and Ned and Lorenzo and Officer Tomilello all looked down at Mercy.

"Are you a thief?" Officer Tomilello asked the man underneath the pig.

"I am," said Leroy Ninker. "I am a thief."

"Were you robbing these people?" Officer Tomilello asked.

"I was," said Leroy Ninker, "until the pig got involved."

"Gentlemen," said Officer Tomilello, "will you assist me in removing the pig?"

On the count of three, Ned and Lorenzo and Officer Tomilello lifted Mercy off of Leroy Ninker.

"You are under arrest," said Officer Tomilello.

"It's that *pig* you should be arresting," said Eugenia Lincoln.

Leroy Ninker stood with his cowboy hat in his hand.

He looked down at his feet.

"Oh, Officer," said Mrs. Watson. "The thief is so tiny. Shouldn't he have something to eat before you arrest him?"

"Maybe he needs some toast," said Ned.

"With a great deal of butter on it," added Lorenzo.

"Toast?" said Officer Tomilello. "Who needs toast?"

"Why, *everyone* needs toast," said Mrs. Watson.

"Even cowboys," said Leroy Ninker.

Mercy pricked up her ears.

Toast!

Butter!

At last!

She headed for the Watsons' kitchen.

And everyone followed her.

Chapter 16

The next morning, the front page of the newspaper read:

PET PIG CAPTURES THIEF

SITS ON HIM UNTIL HELP ARRIVES

"She is a porcine wonder," said the pig's owner, Mrs. Watson.

"She is a very, very brave dear," said Mr. Watson, husband of Mrs. Watson and proud co-owner of the pig.

"She is a sly pig," said the Watsons' neighbor Eugenia Lincoln, "and things with her are never as they seem."

Baby Lincoln, sister to Eugenia Lincoln, remarked that "the most interesting things seem to happen when one has pie right before bed."

"The pig did capture the thief," said police officer Bert Tomilello. "How it happened I am not certain. But did it happen? It did."

Firemen Ned Fortune and Lorenzo Whiz were also at the scene.

They both agreed that the pig had some "amazing abilities."

They also pointed out that Mrs. Watson made excellent toast.

The thief, Leroy Ninker, is interested in reforming himself.

He would like to become a cowboy.

The pig had nothing to say.

But she seemed very pleased with herself.

 **Kate DiCamillo** is the author of *The Tale of Despereaux,* which received the Newbery Medal, *Because of Winn-Dixie,* which received a Newbery Honor, *The Tiger Rising,* which was named a National Book Award Finalist, *The Miraculous Journey of Edward Tulane,* and the Mercy Watson stories. She says, "Happily, Mercy has developed into one of those fabulous characters who is only too pleased to get herself into any number of interesting situations. I just follow her porcine lead." Kate DiCamillo lives in Minnesota.

 **Chris Van Dusen** is the author-illustrator of *A Camping Spree with Mr. Magee* and *If I Built a Car.* He says, "I don't know where Kate comes up with these colorful characters, but I'm thankful that she does, because it makes my job so much fun! When I read that one of the main characters of this book was a very small man/cowboy/thief, I laughed out loud. I based Leroy's look on that of a weasel—long pointy nose, buck teeth, no chin, and huge ears. Even though he's the 'bad guy,' I still love him—as I do all of these characters." Chris Van Dusen lives in Maine.